SUPERMAN
R E T U R N S

Illustrated by Art Mawhinney

Superman created by Jerry Siegel and Joe Shuster

Meredith® Books
Des Moines, Iowa

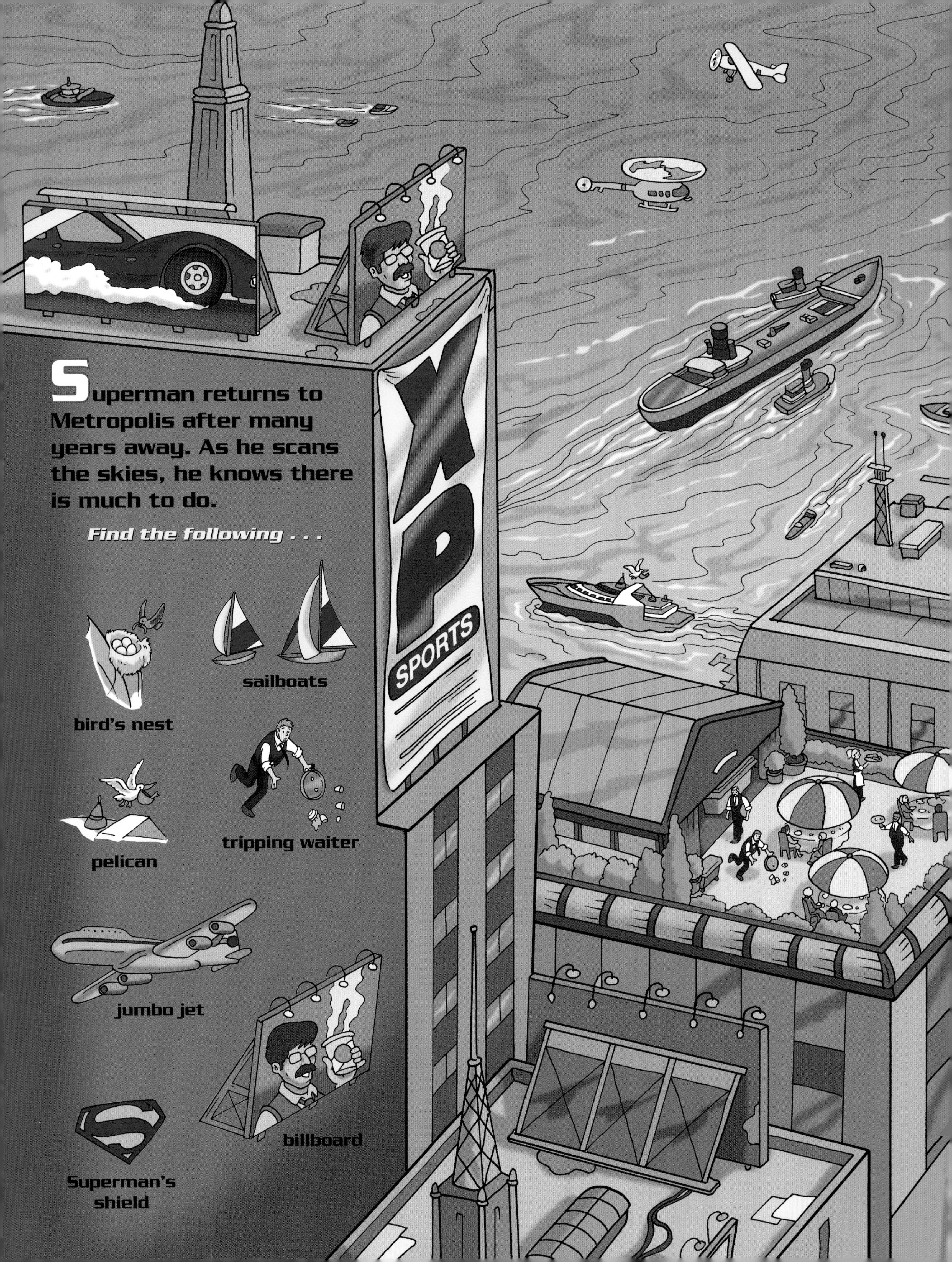

Superman returns to Metropolis after many years away. As he scans the skies, he knows there is much to do.
Find the following . . .
sailboats
bird's nest
pelican
tripping waiter
jumbo jet
billboard
Superman's shield
XP
SPORTS

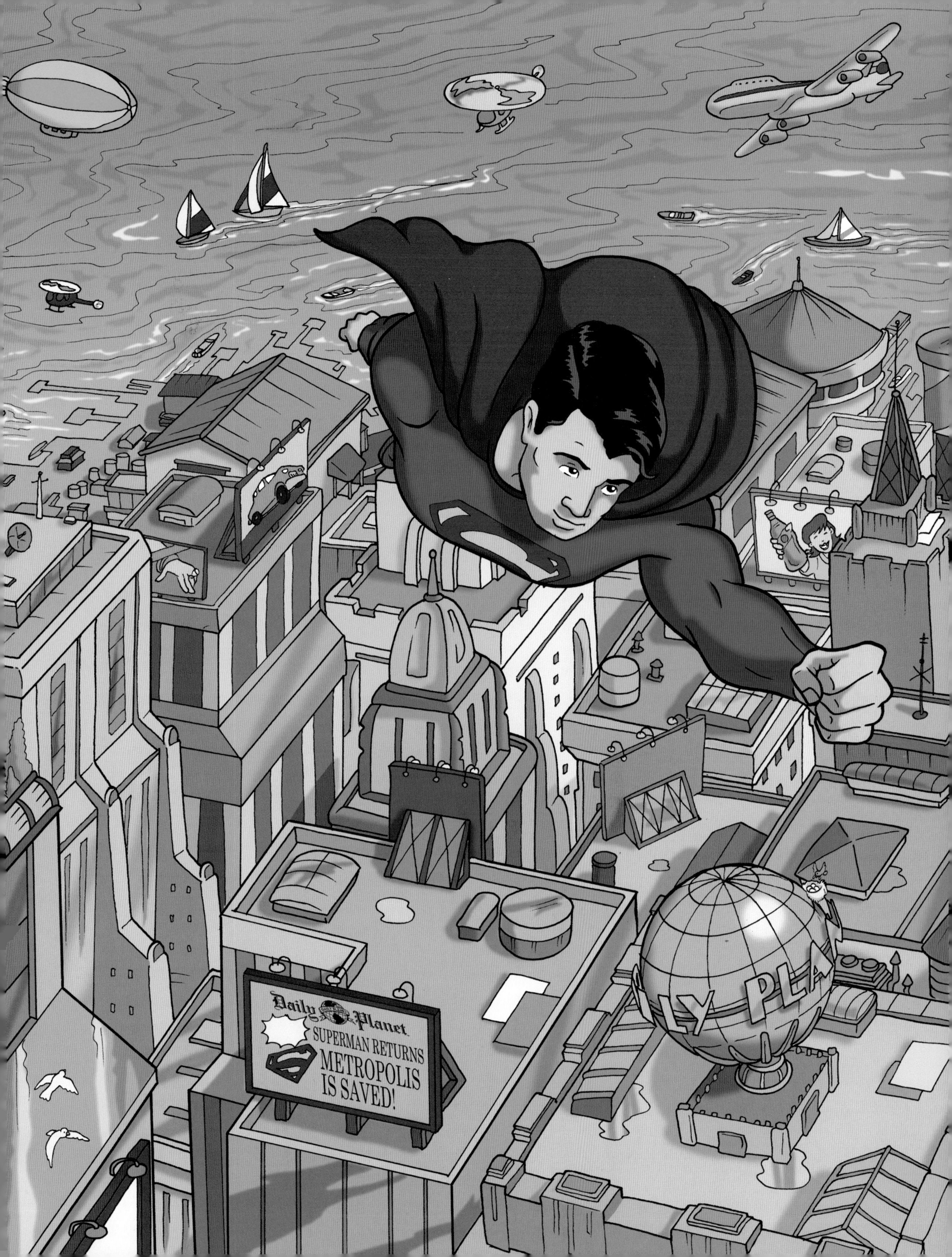
Daily Planet
SUPERMAN RETURNS
METROPOLIS
IS SAVED!

Superman spies a bank robbery in progress and swoops down to stop the thieves.

Find the following . . .

- bag of money
- police officer
- Superman's shield
- impressed pedestrian
- bank teller
- police car

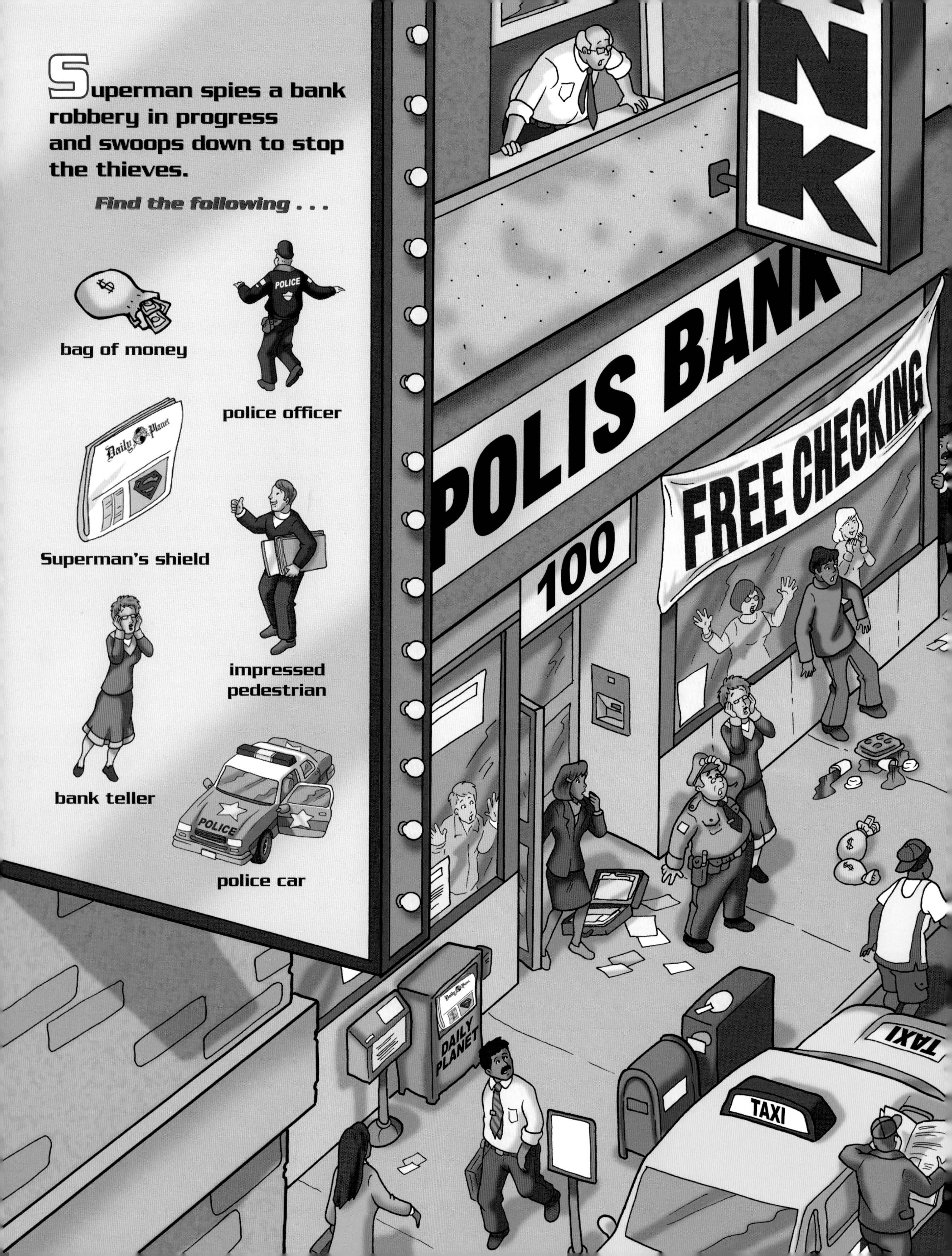

POLICE
Daily Planet
POLICE
NK
POLIS BANK
FREE CHECKING
100
DAILY PLANET
TAXI
TAXI

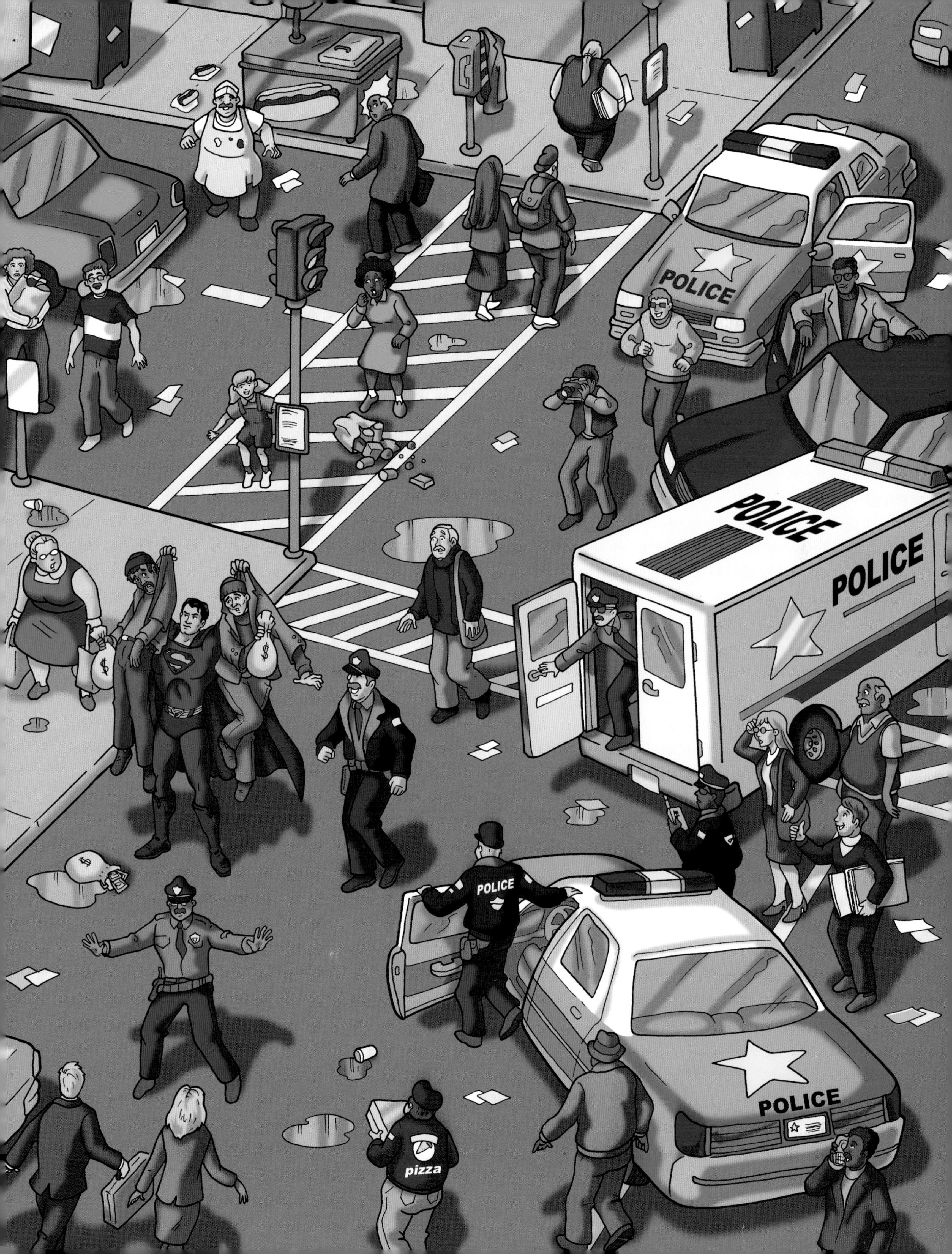
POLICE
POLICE
POLICE
POLICE
POLICE
POLICE
pizza

Capturing the bank robbers has made Superman late for work. He ducks into a quiet alley and changes into his secret identity of Clark Kent.

Find the following . . .

- Superman's shield
- Krypton Kola
- Clark's glasses
- alley cats
- happy dog
- *Daily Planet*

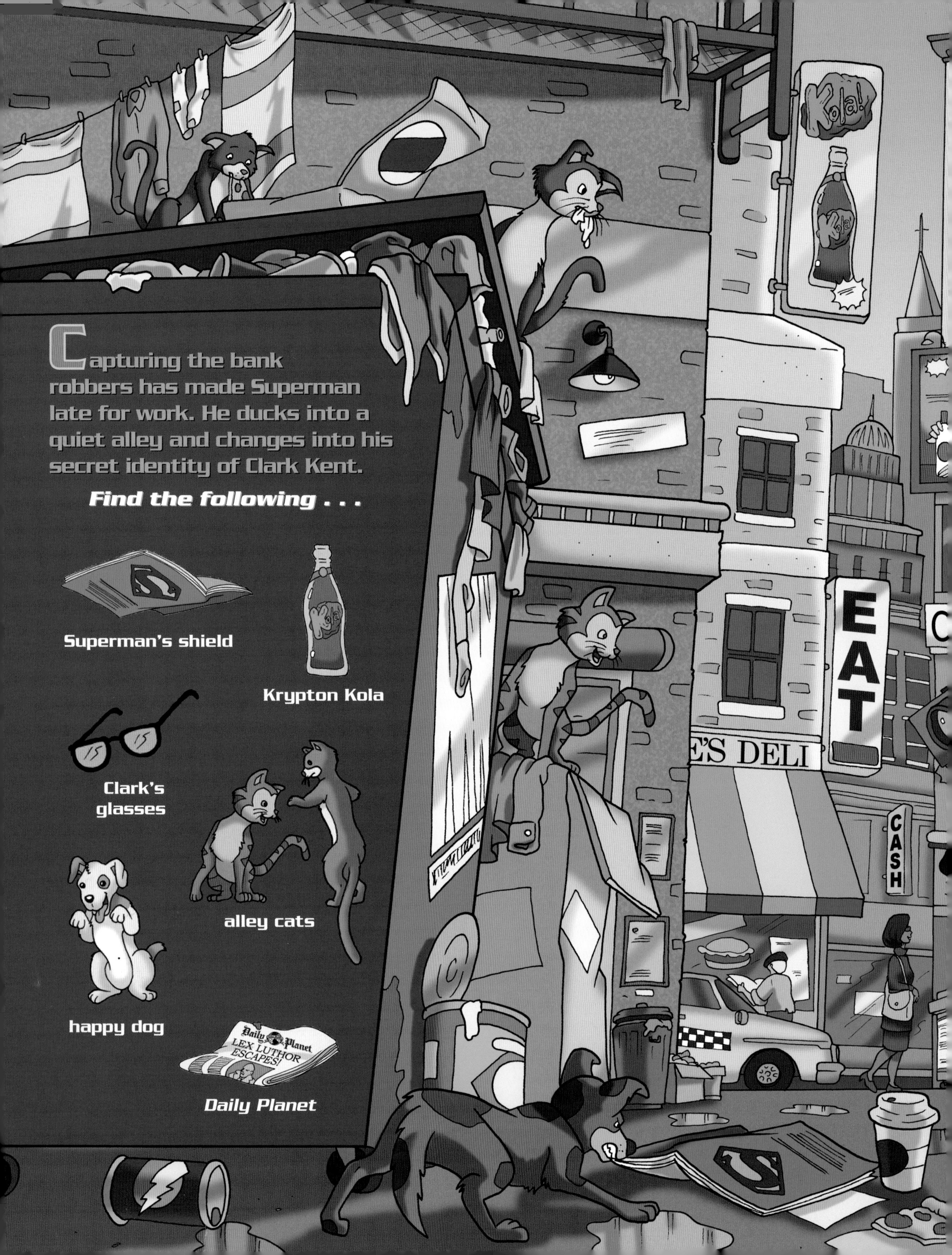
Kola!
Kola
Daily Planet
LEX LUTHOR ESCAPES!
EAT
'S DELI
CASH

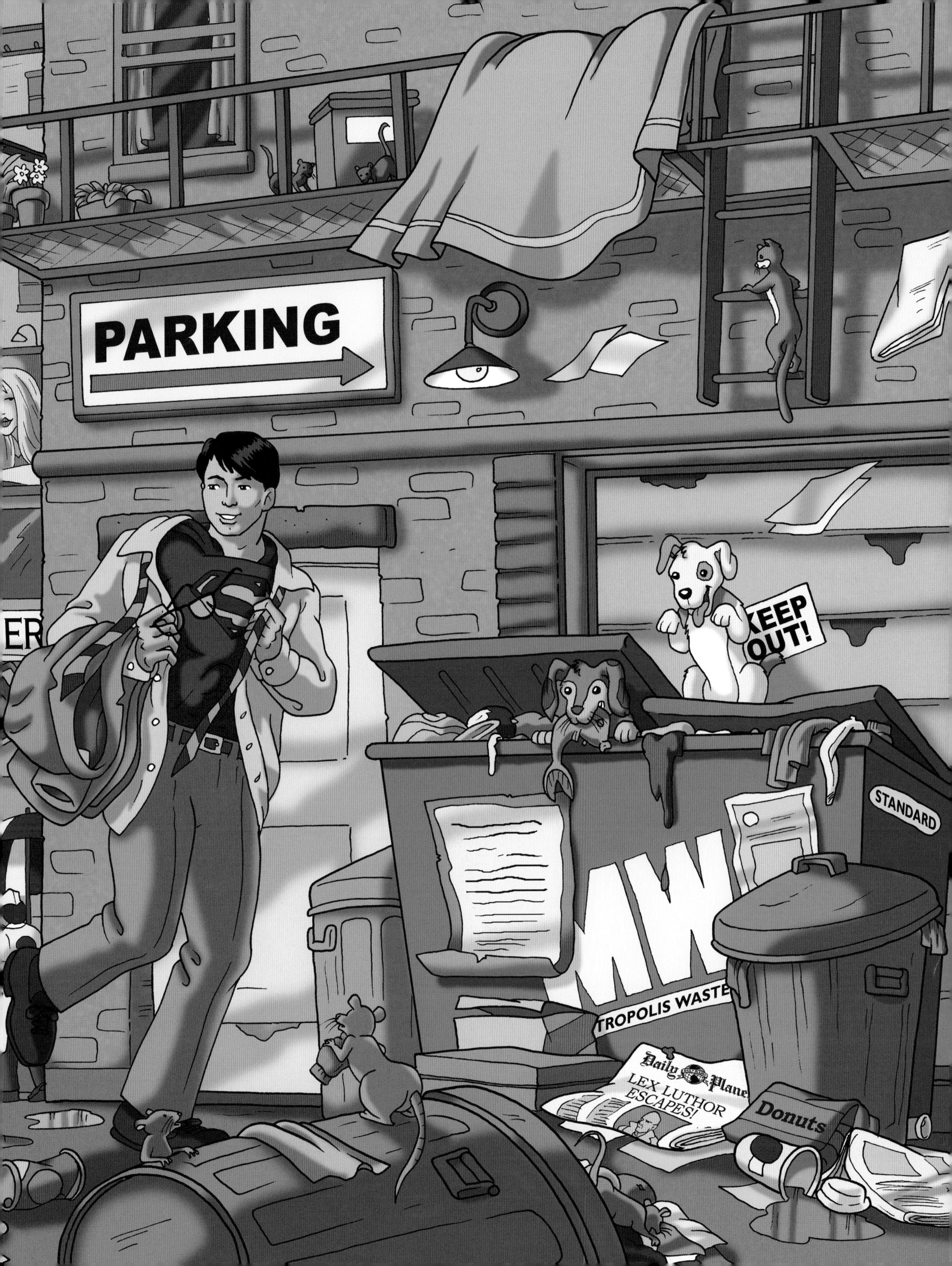
PARKING
KEEP OUT!
STANDARD
MW
TROPOLIS WASTE
Daily Plane
LEX LUTHOR ESCAPES!
Donuts

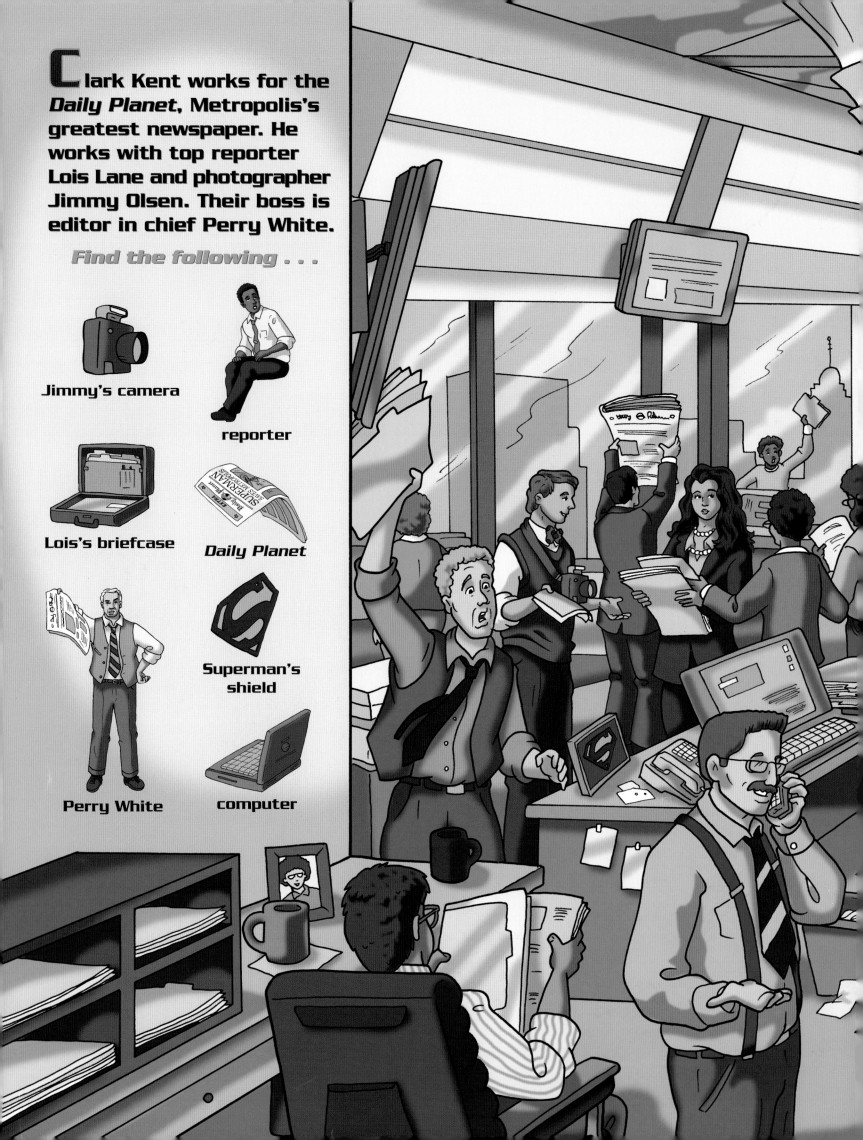

Clark Kent works for the *Daily Planet*, Metropolis's greatest newspaper. He works with top reporter Lois Lane and photographer Jimmy Olsen. Their boss is editor in chief Perry White.

Find the following . . .

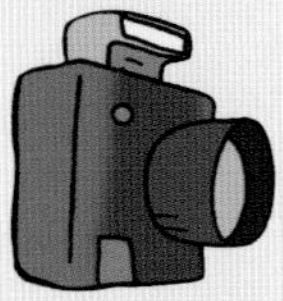

Jimmy's camera

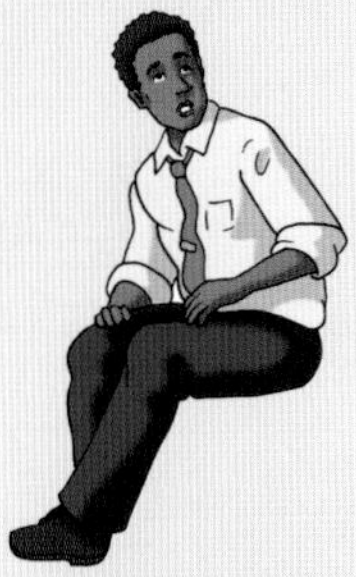

reporter

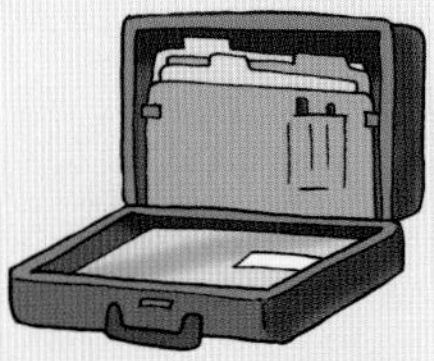

Lois's briefcase

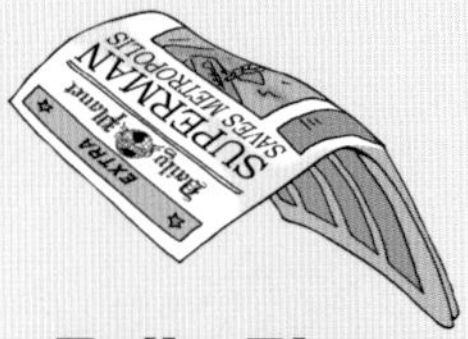

Daily Planet

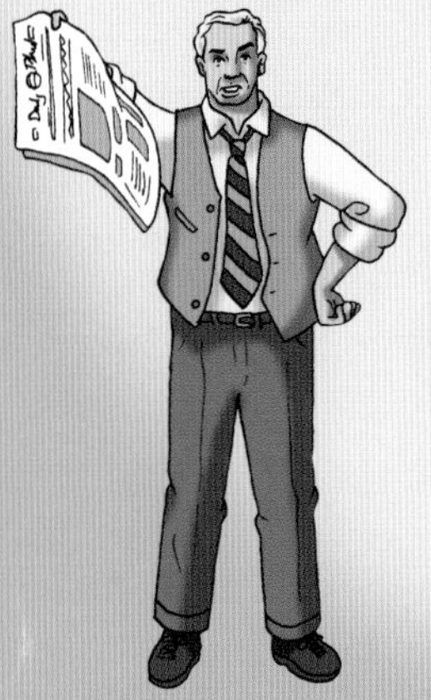

Perry White

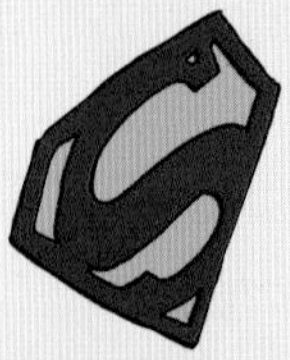

Superman's shield

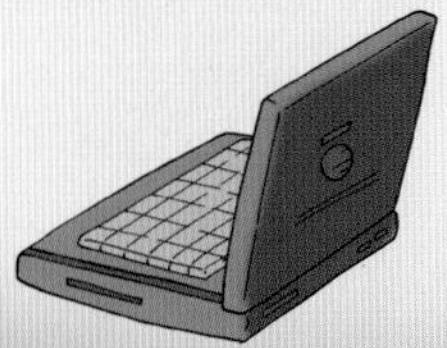

computer

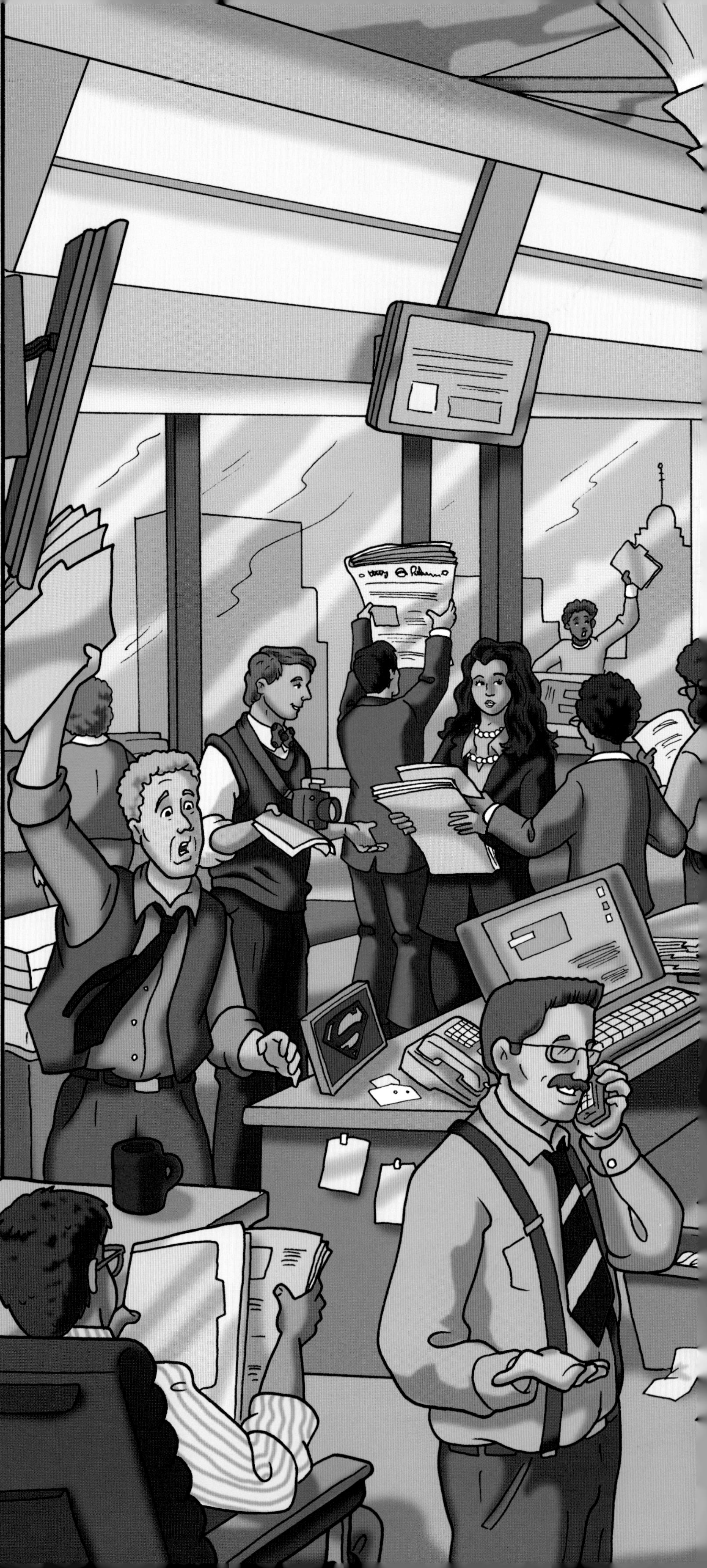

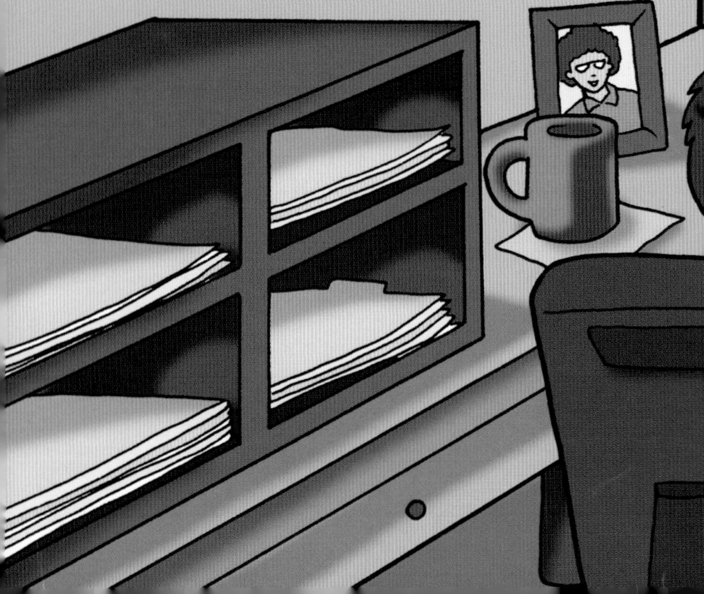

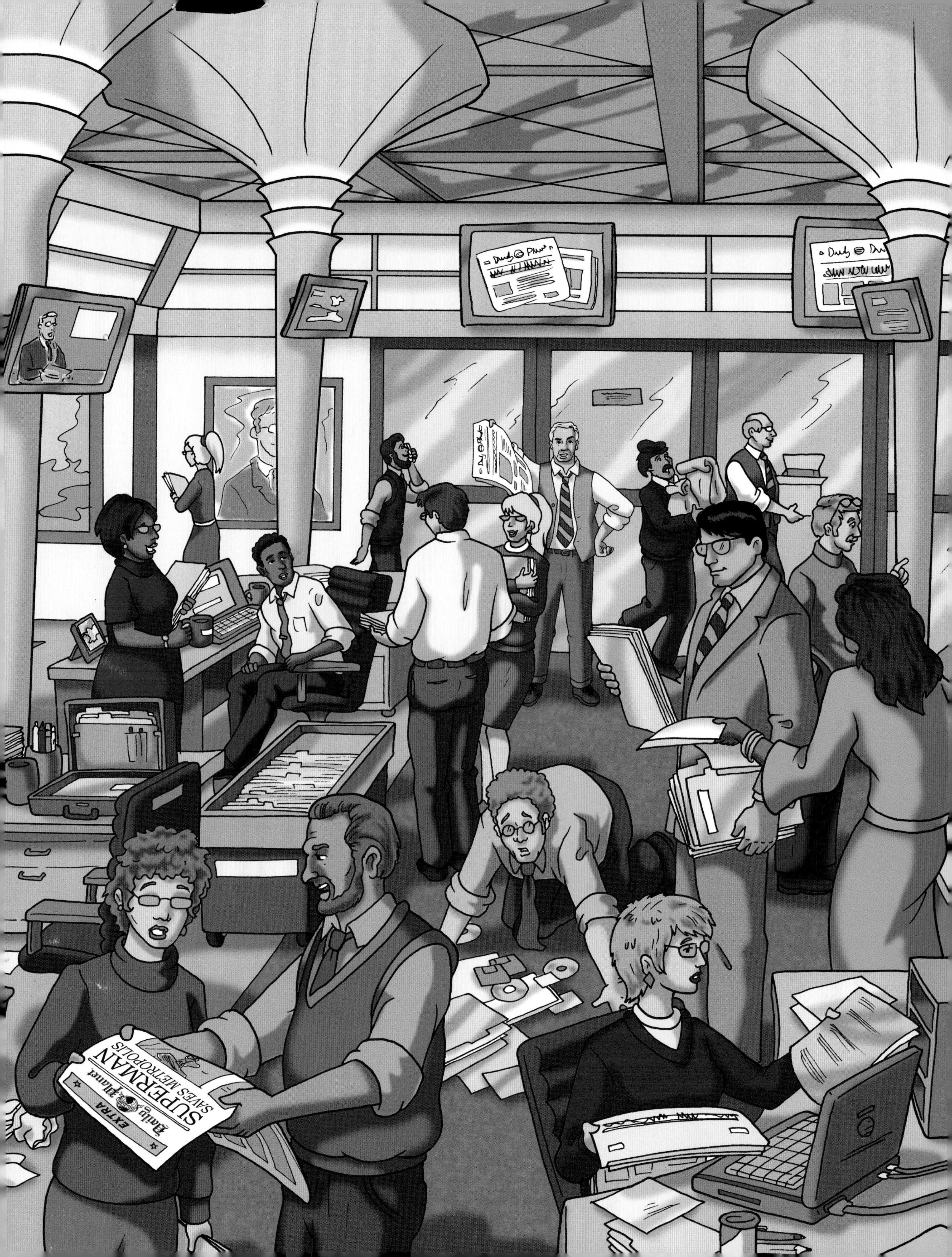
EXTRA
Daily Planet
SUPERMAN
SAVES METROPOLIS

But Superman's job is never done! He must leave work to help rescue a baby panda at Metropolis Zoo . . .

Find the following . . .

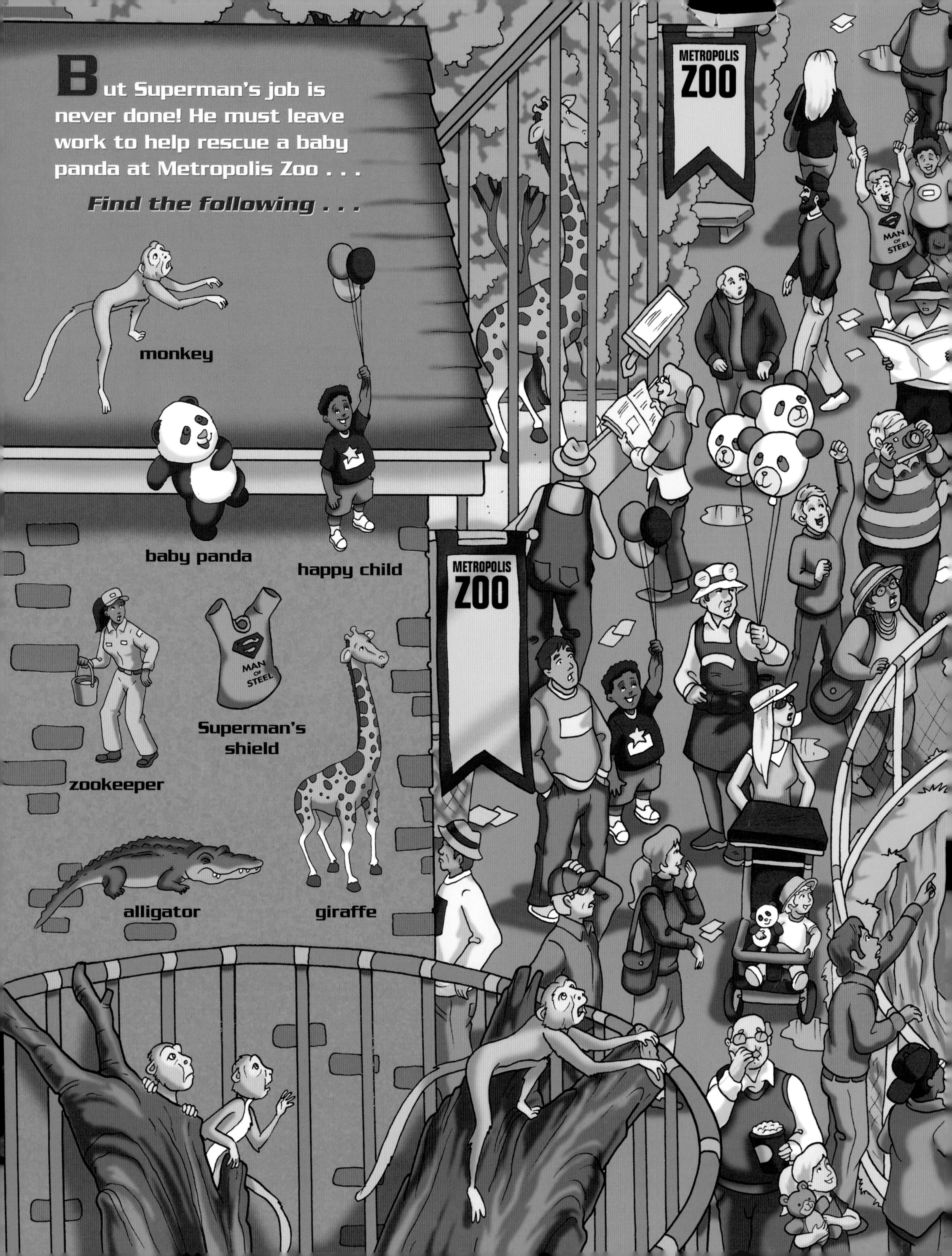
monkey
baby panda
happy child
zookeeper
Superman's shield
MAN OF STEEL
alligator
giraffe
METROPOLIS ZOO
METROPOLIS ZOO

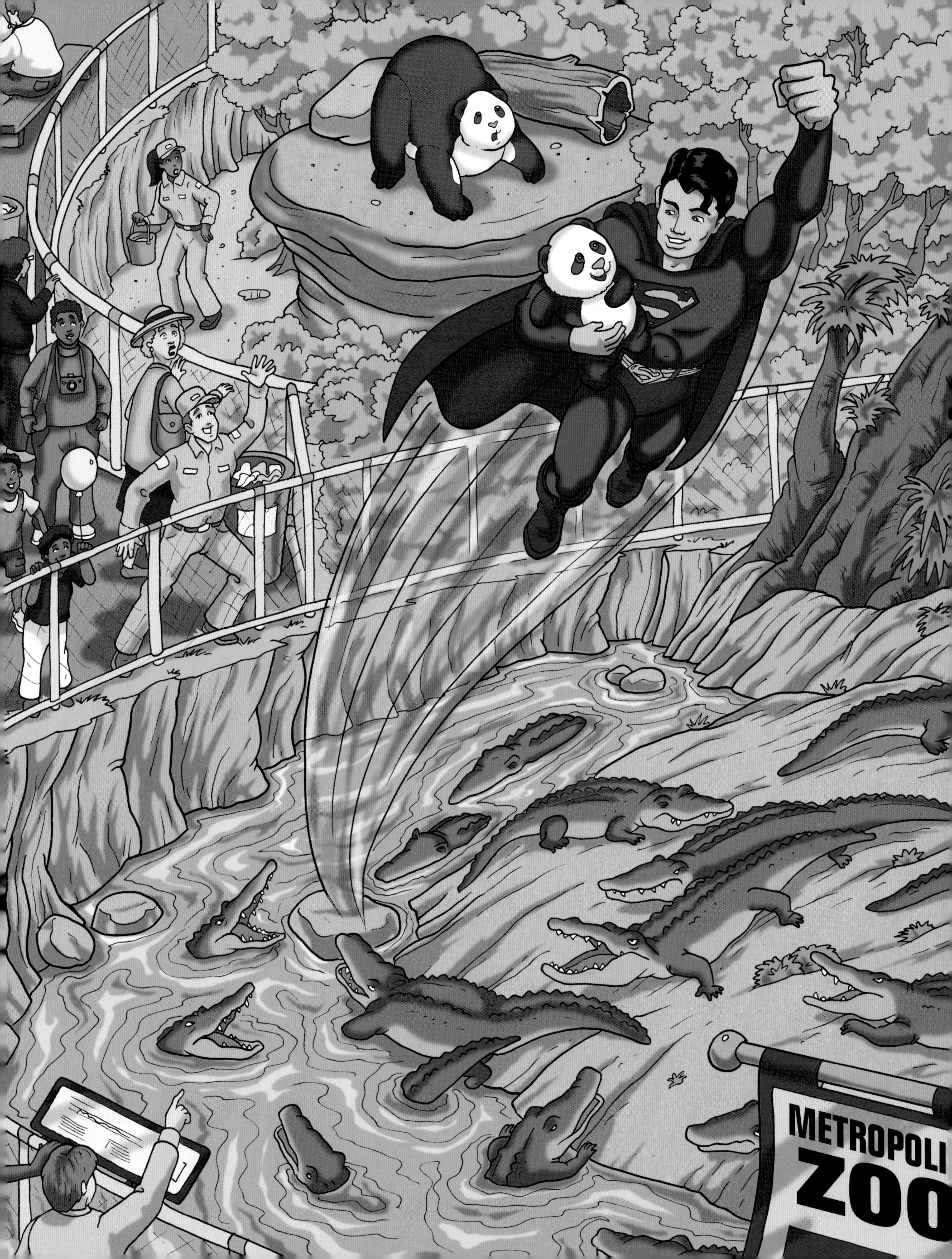
METROPOLI
ZOO

. . . and help the Metropolis Fire Department put out a fire . . .

Find the following . . .

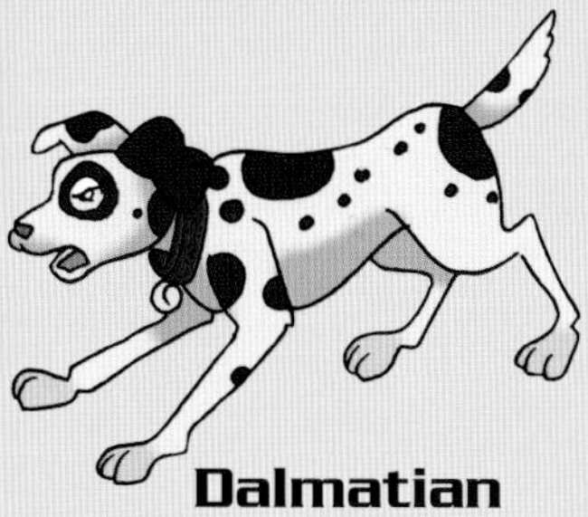

Dalmatian

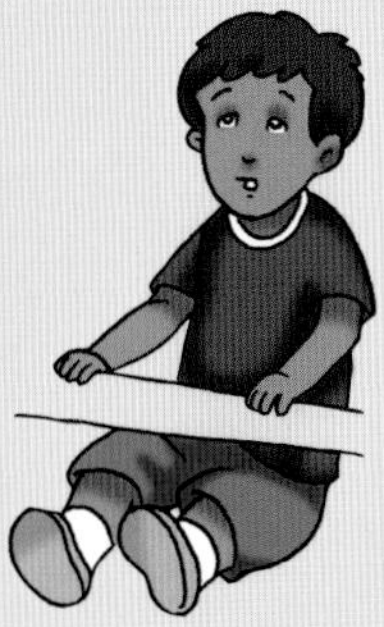

child

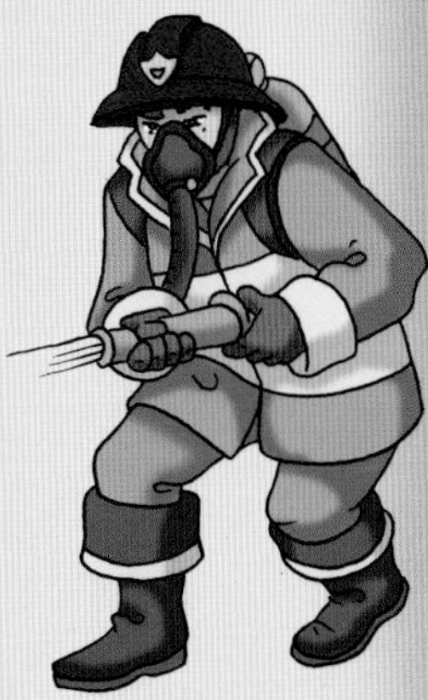

firefighter

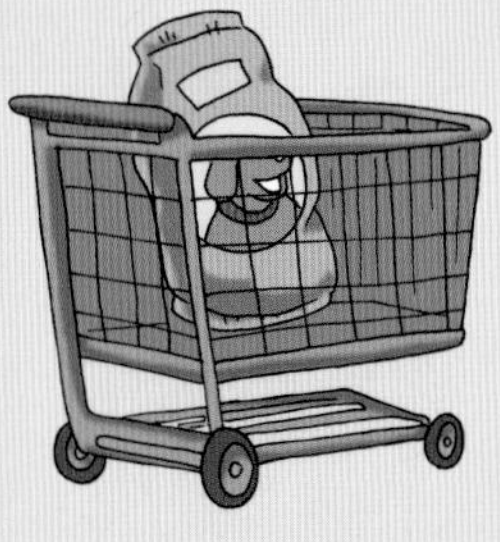

shopping cart

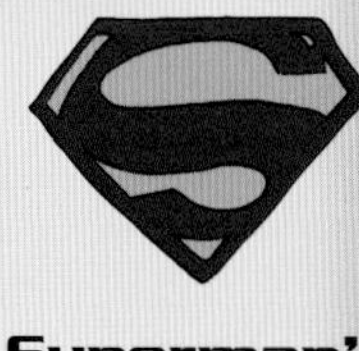

Superman's shield

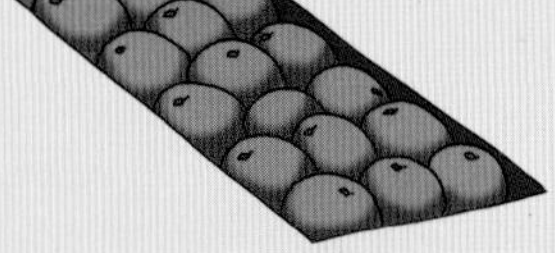

box of oranges

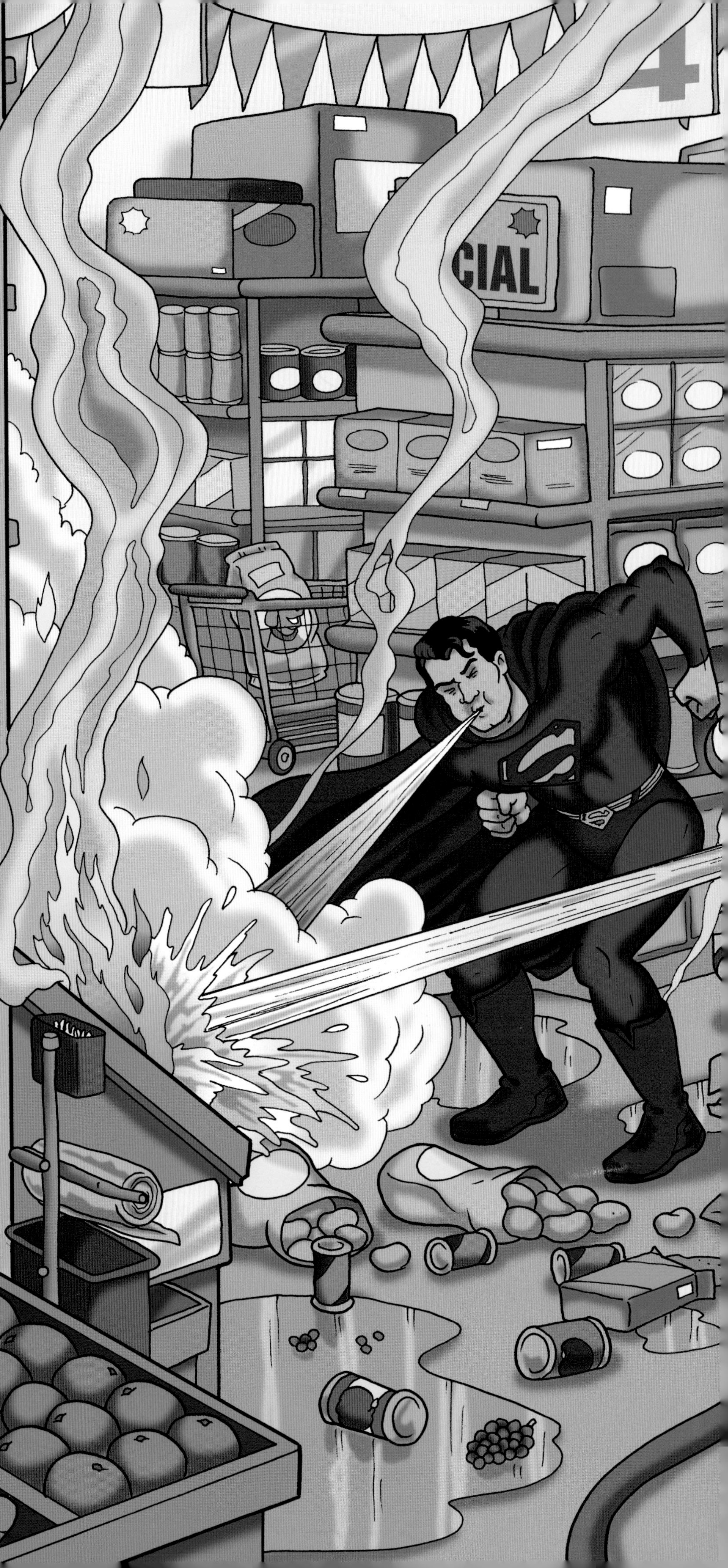
CIAL
Zucchini
Oranges

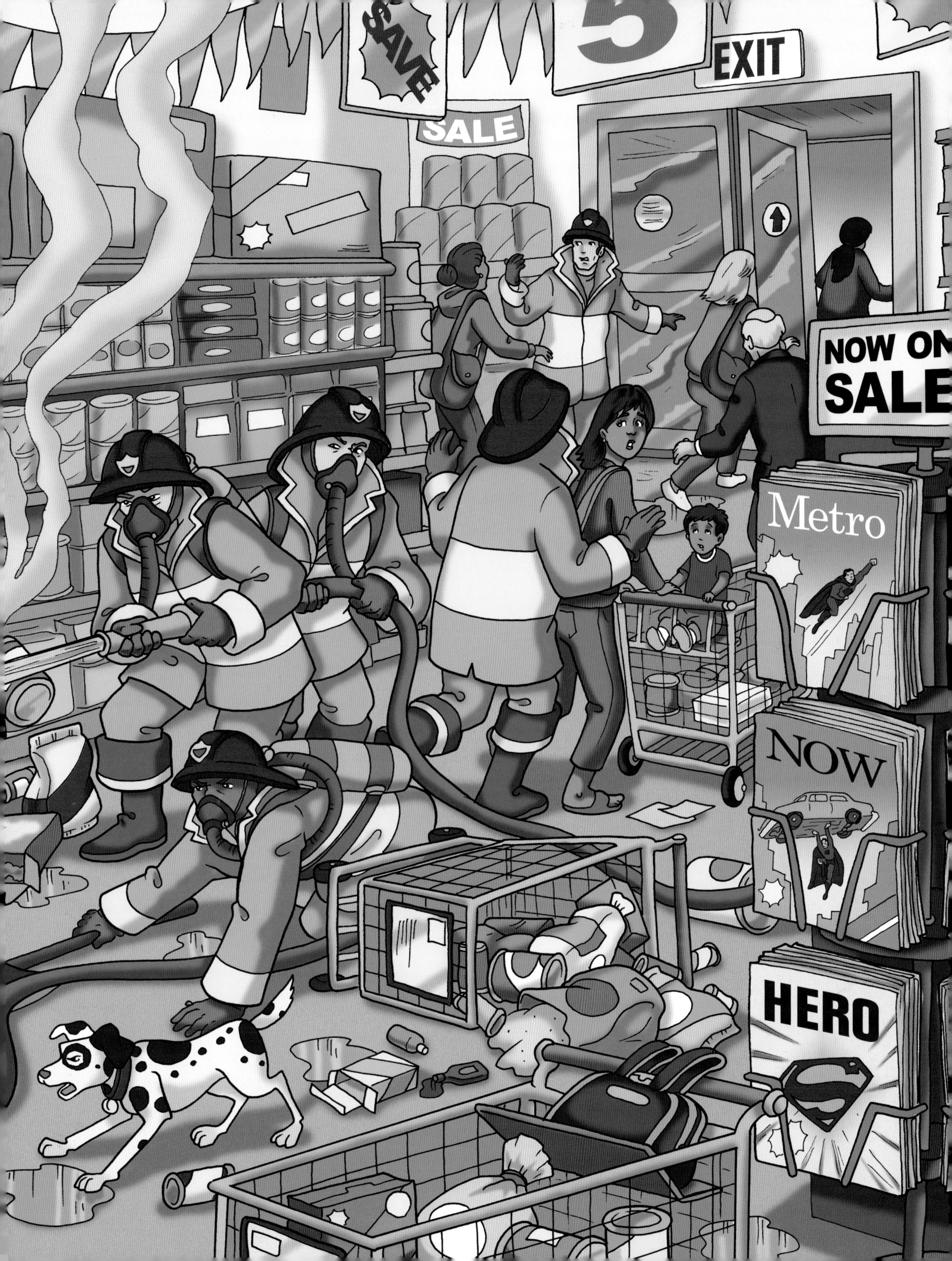
SAVE
SALE
EXIT
NOW ON
SALE
Metro
NOW
HERO

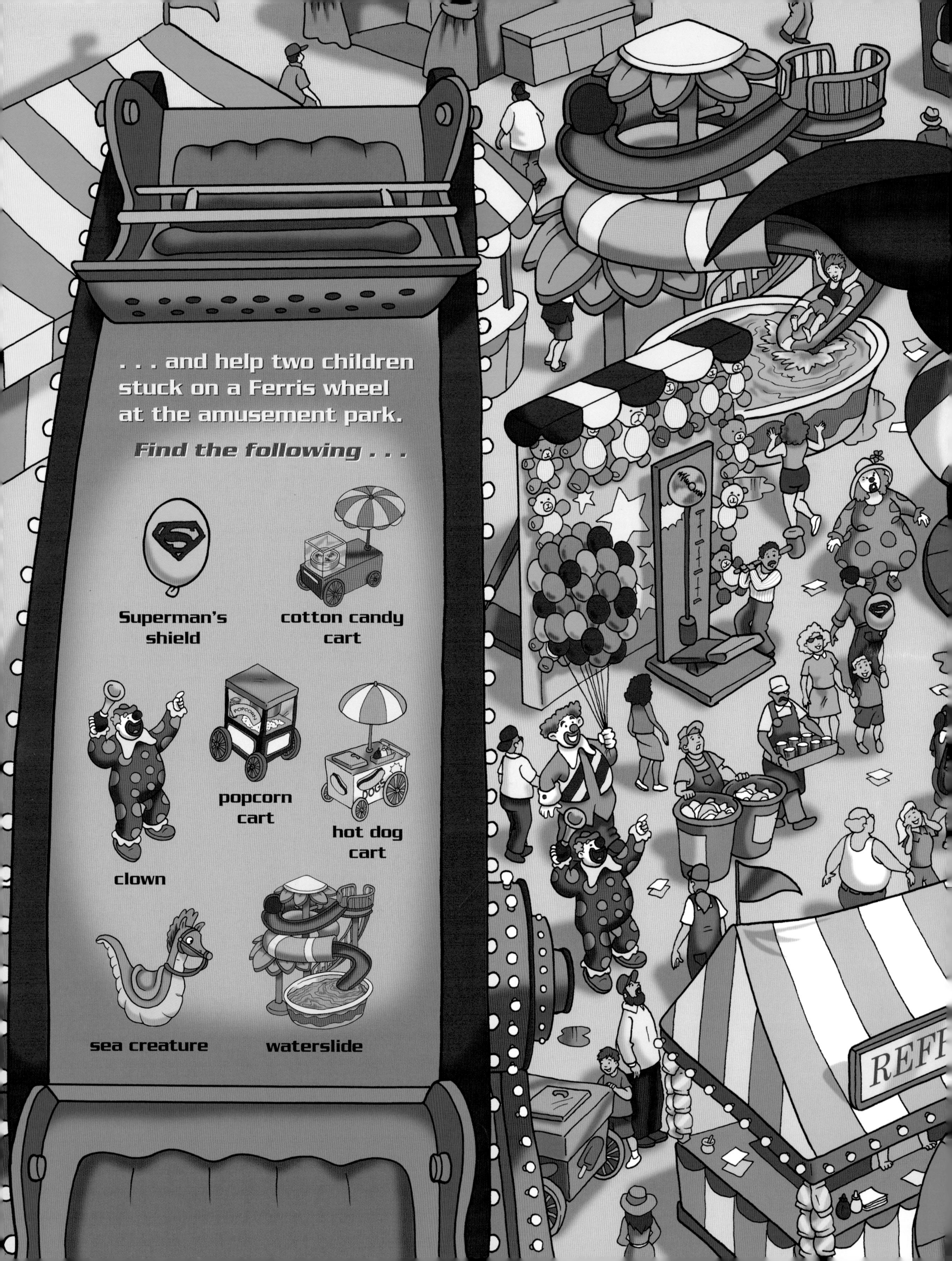

. . . and help two children stuck on a Ferris wheel at the amusement park.
Find the following . . .
Superman's shield
cotton candy cart
clown
popcorn cart
POPCORN
hot dog cart
DOGS
sea creature
waterslide

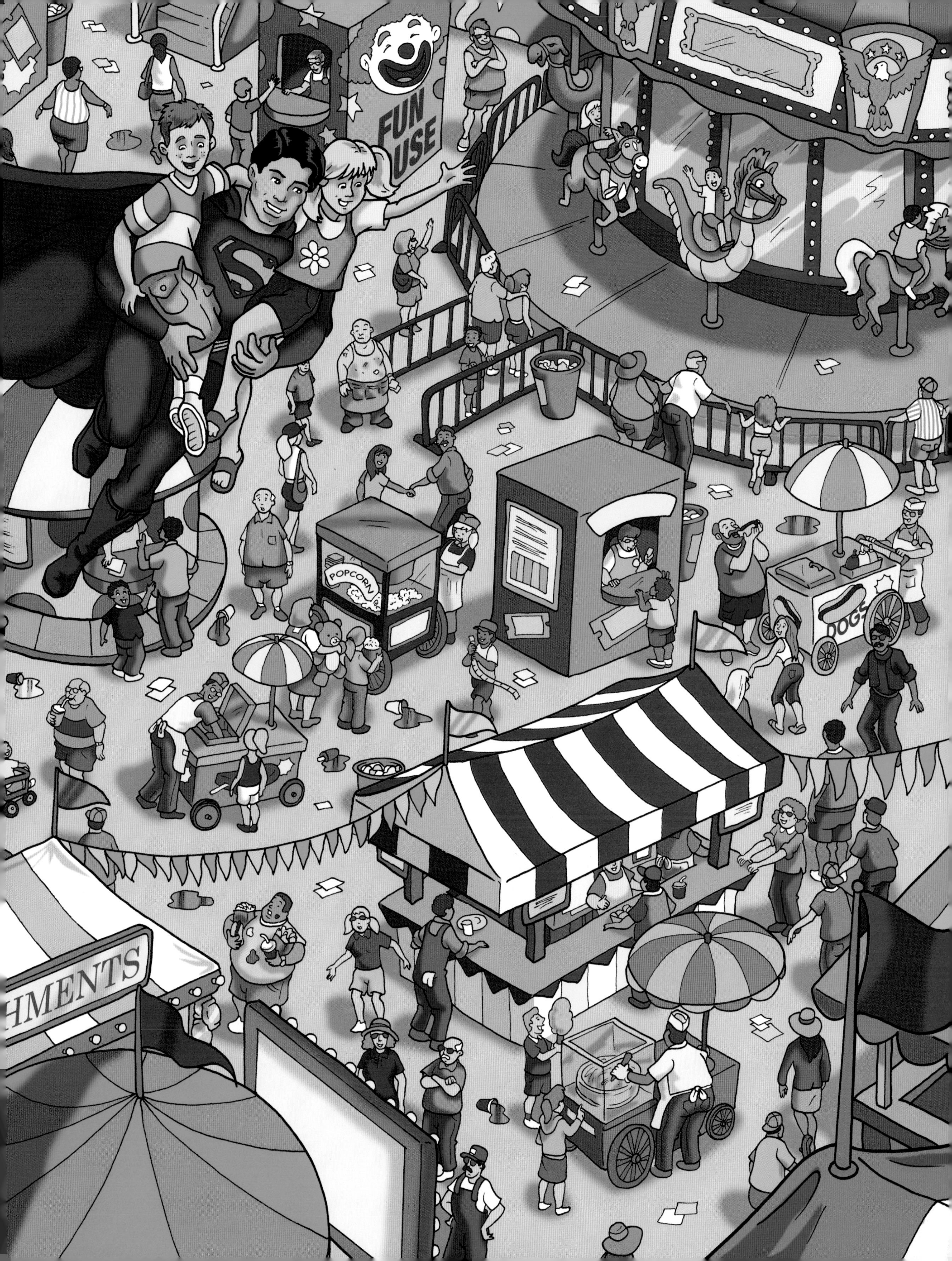
FUN
USE
POPCORN
DOGS
HMENTS

Superman also takes the time to help those who need a friend.

Find the following . . .

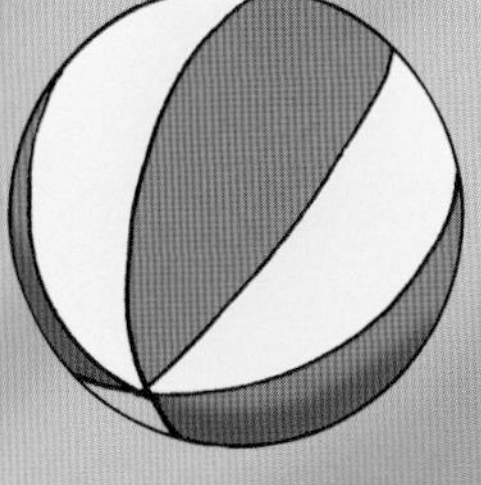

beach ball

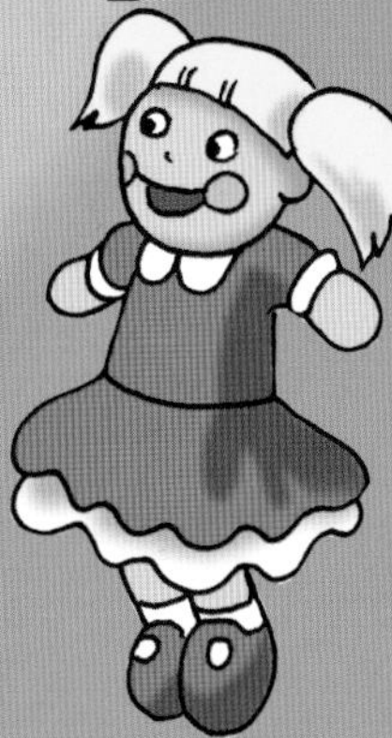

baby doll

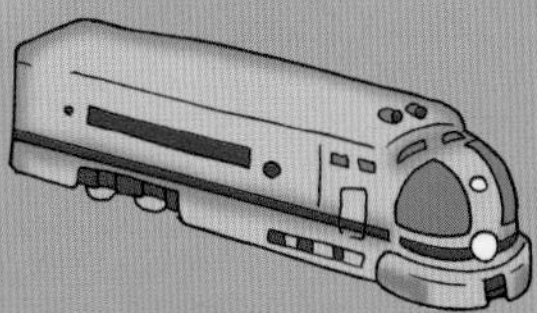

train set

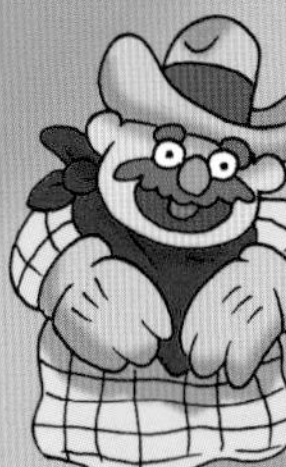

cowboy puppet

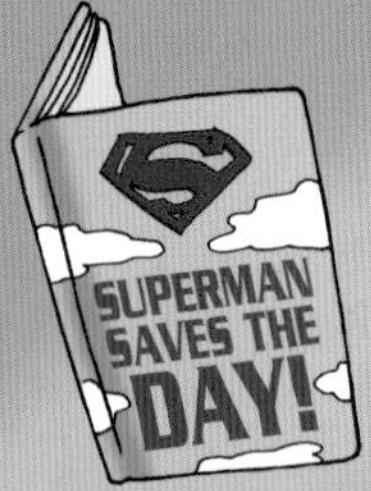
SUPERMAN SAVES THE DAY!

Superman's shield

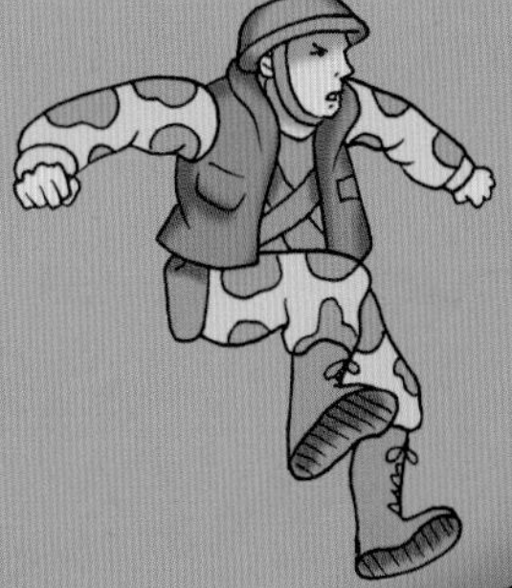

toy soldier

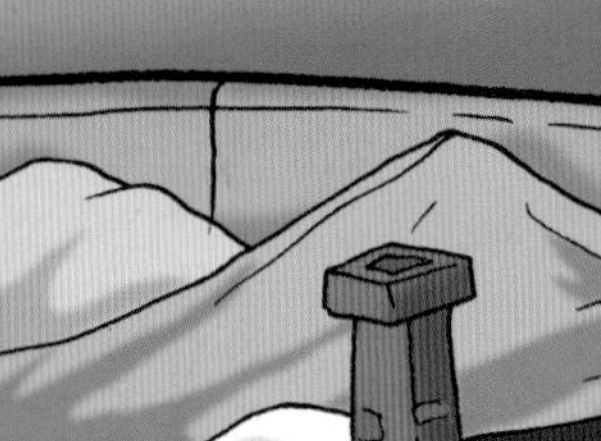

fire truck

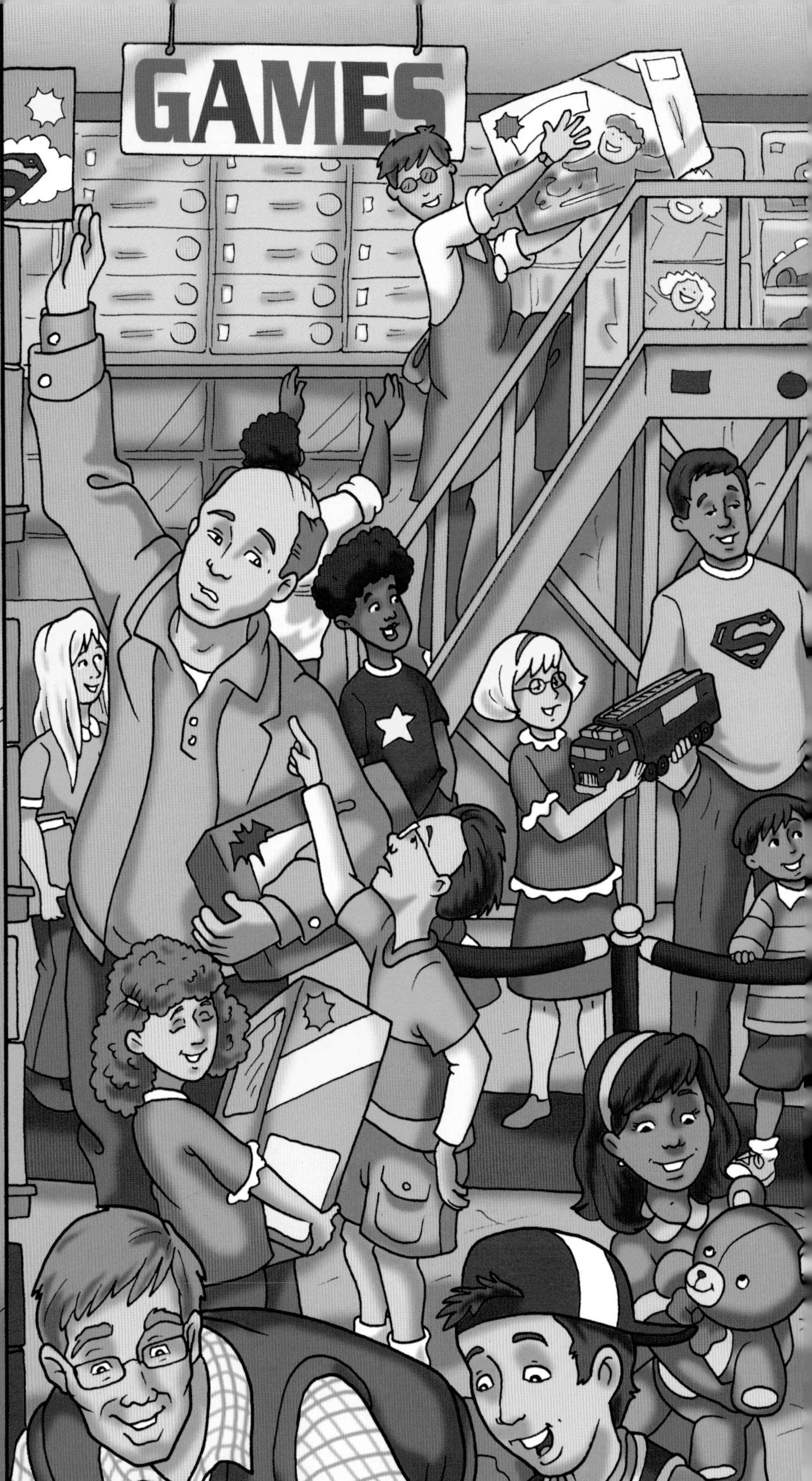
GAMES

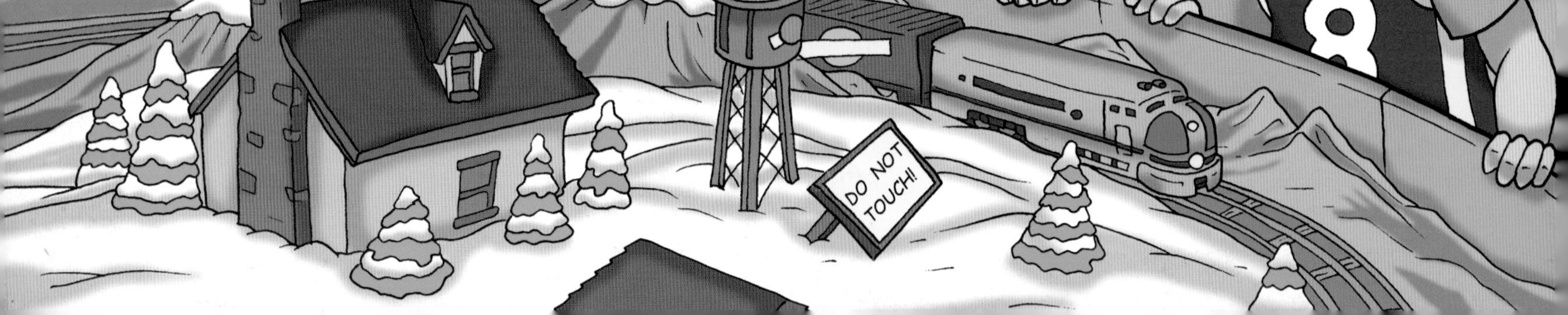
8
DO NOT TOUCH!

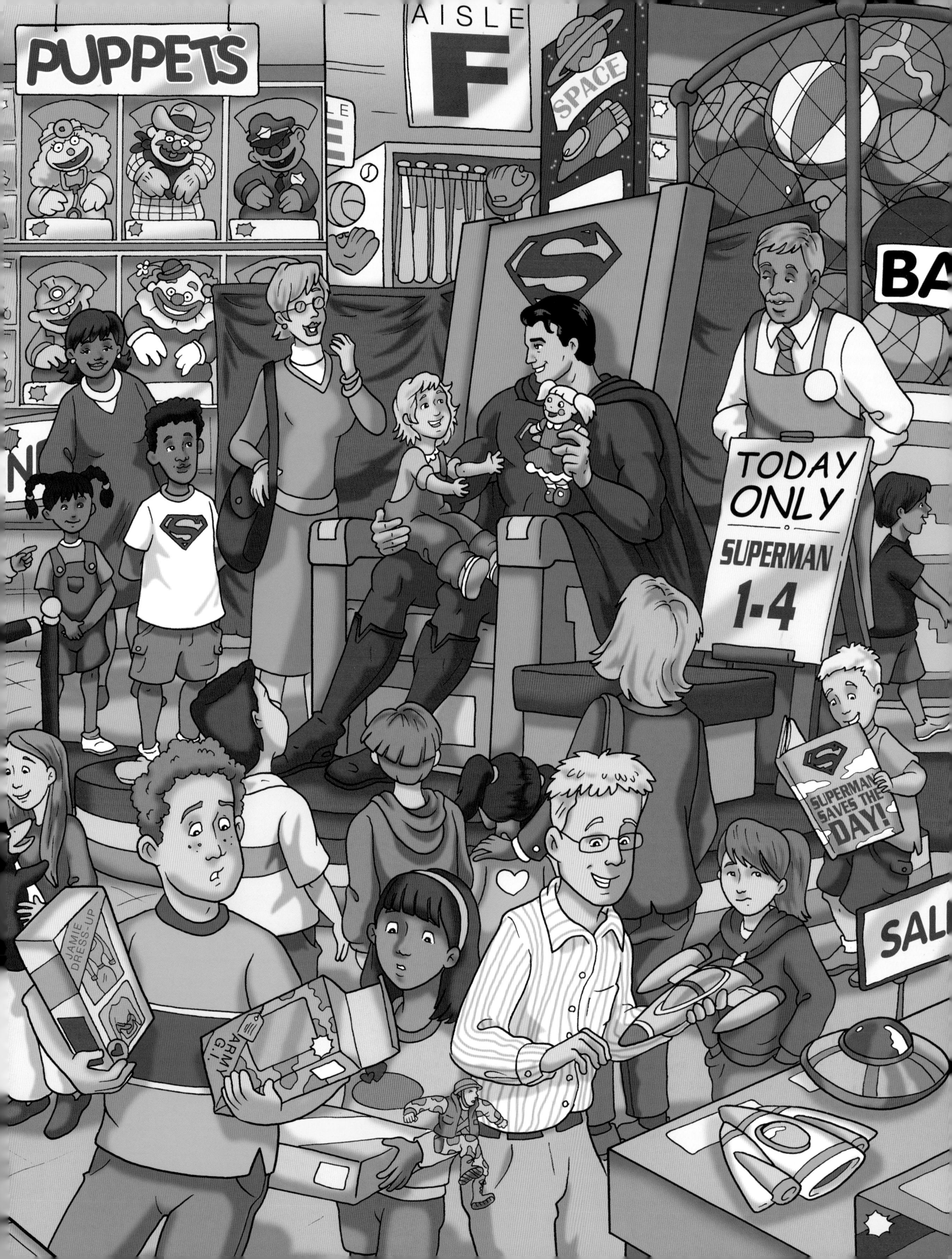
PUPPETS
AISLE
F
SPACE
TODAY ONLY
SUPERMAN
1-4
SUPERMAN SAVES THE DAY!
JAMIE DRESS-UP
ARMY G.I.

Sometimes he even has to help those he cares about most. Lois Lane often gets into trouble, but that's her job as a reporter!

Find the following . . .

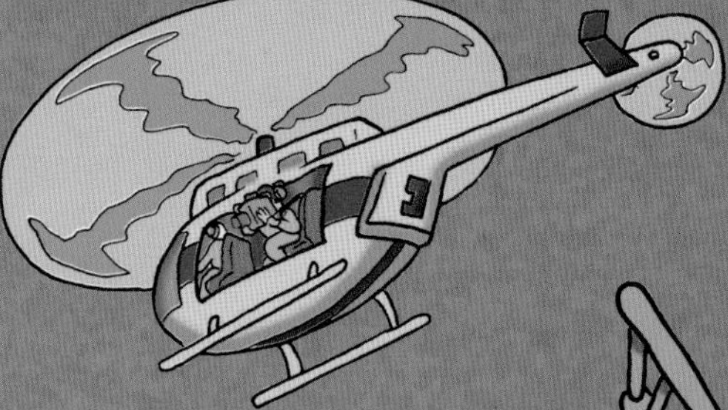

helicopter

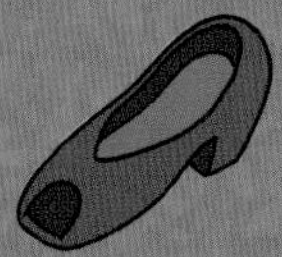

lost shoe

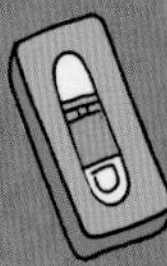

recorder

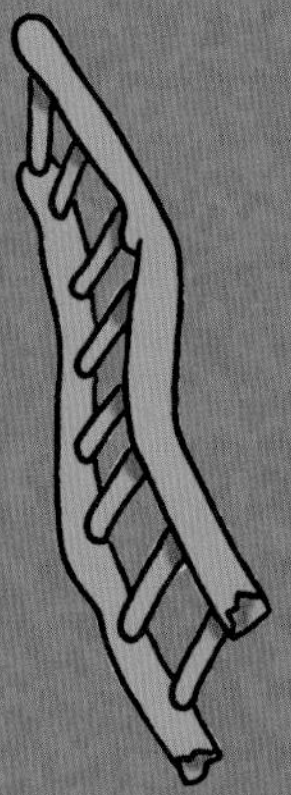

broken rail

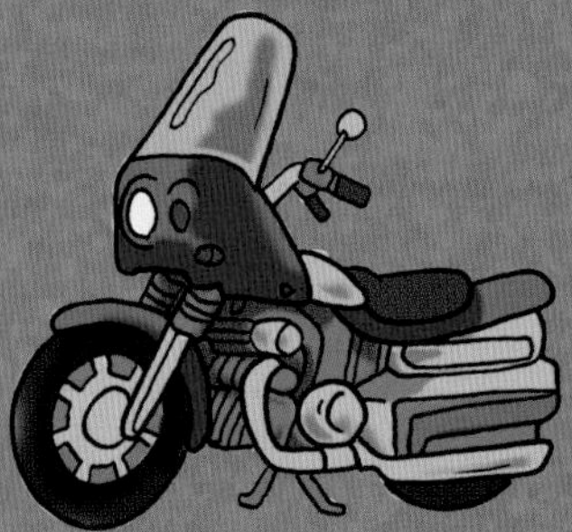

police motorcycle

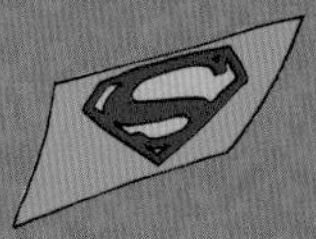

Superman's shield

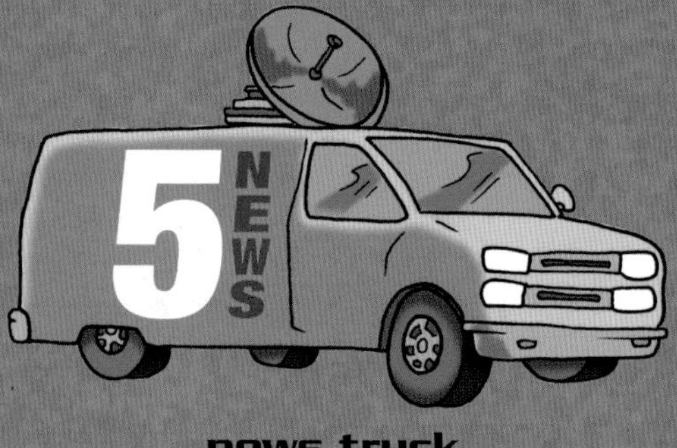
5 NEWS

news truck

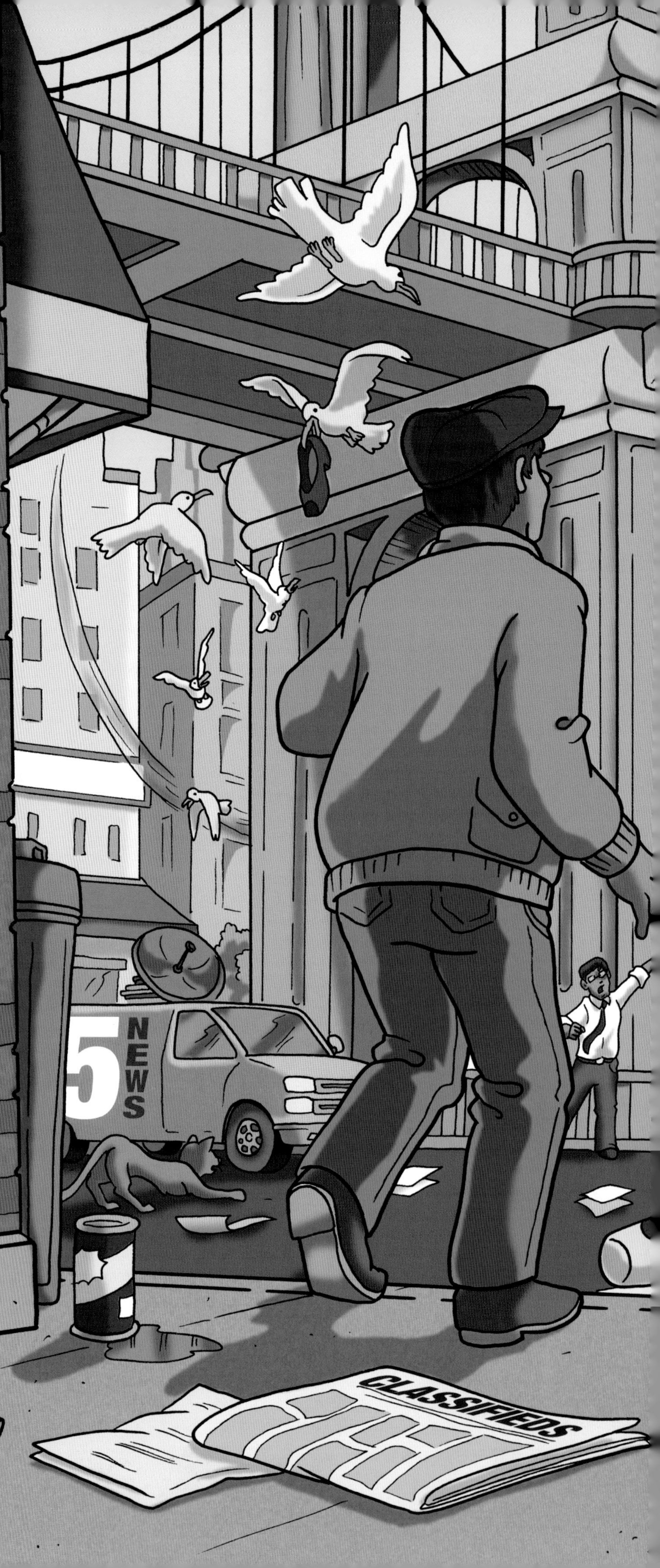
5 NEWS
CLASSIFIEDS

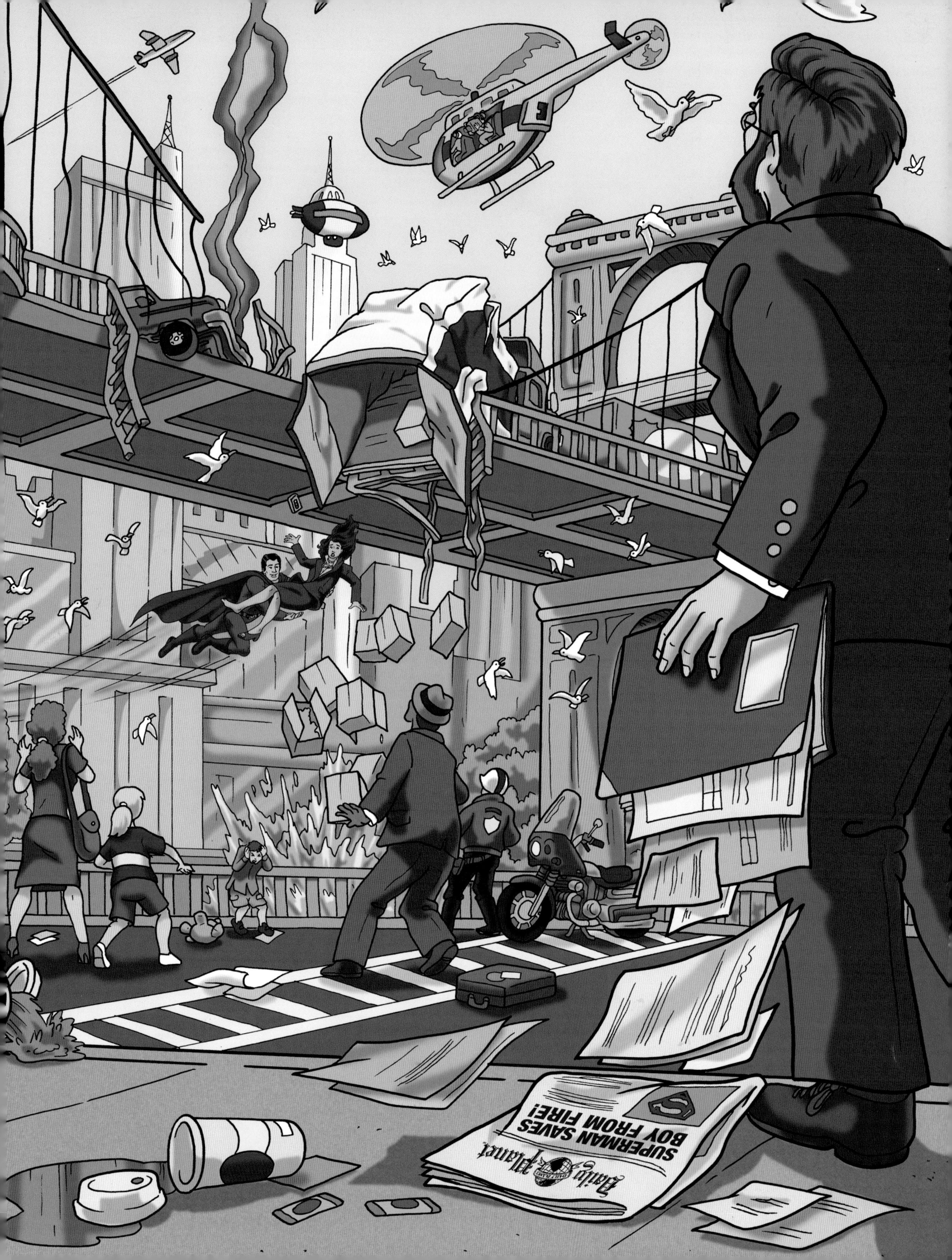
Daily Planet
SUPERMAN SAVES
BOY FROM FIRE!

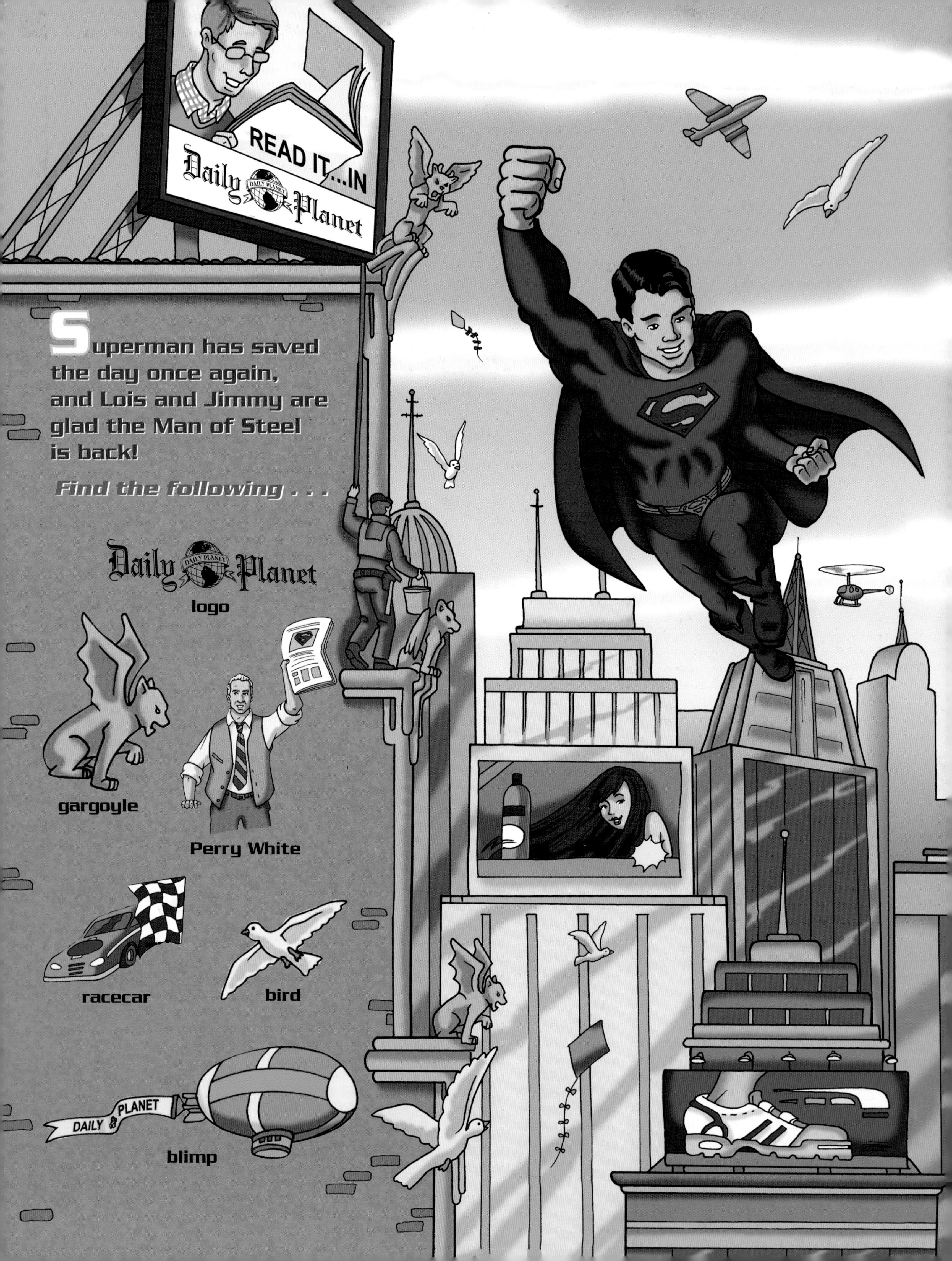
READ IT...IN
Daily Planet
Superman has saved the day once again, and Lois and Jimmy are glad the Man of Steel is back!
Find the following . . .
Daily Planet
logo
gargoyle
Perry White
racecar
bird
DAILY PLANET
blimp